FEAR OF RAIN

A Johnstown Tale

ROBERT JESCHONEK

pie
press

FEAR OF RAIN

A Pie Press book

pie press publishing

Published by Pie Press Publishing
411 Chancellor Street
Johnstown, Pennsylvania 15904
www.piepresspublishing.com

A Glosser's Christmas Love Story

Christmas at Glosser's

Death by Polka

Easter at Glosser's

Fear of Rain

Fourth of July at Glosser's

Halloween at Glosser's

Long Live Glosser's

Old-Fashioned Bargain Days at Glosser's

Penn Traffic Forever

Richland Mall Rules

Thanksgiving at Glosser's

The Glory of Gable's

The Masked Family

Valentine's Day at Glosser's

Mr. Flood bangs his fork on the side of his plate, and thunder rumbles outside the restaurant. He winks one watery, sky blue eye at me and peels back his smooth, white lips in a dirty joke smile.

"Won't be long now," he says, his voice a gravelly tenor. "Not long till my retirement party."

If you didn't know better, to look at him, you'd think he was just another little old man hobbling around downtown Johnstown, Pennsylvania. Just another Central Park bench sitting, Social Security check cashing, prescription picking up, stumbling on the curbs, taking too long to cross Main Street old timer. You'd never know the kind of power that boils inside him.

Maybe you'd see him bang his fork on the plate a second time, and you'd hear the thunder, louder than before, but you wouldn't connect the two. You wouldn't realize that he'd made it happen. You wouldn't know what he was about to do next.

But I know. I know all about what's coming.

It's the Big Night. He's wearing his lucky suit for the occasion--a powder blue leisure suit from the '70's with white piping around the collar, lapels, and pockets.

He's the closest thing I have to a father, and I'm part of this, too. Tonight's his retirement party and my graduation party wrapped up in one...though the people of Johnstown will call it something different altogether.

The ones who survive, anyway.

"I just hope I'm ready," I say, picking at the gray, gravy-drowned meat loaf on my own cracked plate. Mr. Flood has wolfed down his turkey dinner like a teenage football star and chased it with a double slice of graham cracker pie, but I'm way too nervous tonight to be hungry.

"You're more ready than I was in '36, Dee," says Mr. Flood, wagging his chicken hawk head on a neck so wishbone scrawny it looks like it ought to snap in two any second now. "I wasn't nearly as good a student as you, and look how that turned out! Seventeen feet of water!"

I shrug and sigh and twist my curly, black hair around my index finger. I know my whole eighteen years of life have been leading up to this night, but now that it's here, I kind of wish that it wasn't. "Stressed out" doesn't begin to cover the way I feel.

You'd be stressed out, too, if you were about to help destroy a city.

"Now drink up," says Mr. Flood, refilling my water glass from the pitcher that he had the waitress leave at the table. The ice chips tinkle as he pushes the sweating glass toward me. "It's almost time."

Him and his water drinking, I think, but then I do what I've done all my life, which is what he tells me. I already have to pee like crazy, but I still gulp down half the glass.

I can't even think about slipping off to the ladies' room. A full bladder is part of the magic, Mr. Flood always says. Filling yourself with water till you're ready to explode.

And then you do the same thing to the sky.

Mr. Flood refills my glass to the brim, and I roll my eyes, but I have another big drink. He just lifts the whole pitcher to his lips then, and it's maybe half full, and he chugs it.

Except for a little bit left in the bottom, which he swishes around a few times and then slowly pours out on the table.

The water trickles from the rim of the sideways turned pitcher and patters on the sticky, dull wood of the tabletop.

And at the same moment, the same exact moment, I hear it start to rain outside.

"One two, buckle my shoe," says Mr. Flood. "Three four, let it pour."

And that's how it starts. No one will ever know except me and Mr. Flood, but that's exactly how the whole thing starts.

The fourth Johnstown Flood.

"Check, please," he says to the ragged waitress.

OUTSIDE, I POP AN UMBRELLA, BECAUSE IT'S REALLY coming down, but Mr. Flood takes it away from me.

"Now who ever heard of a Flood using an umbrella?" he says disgustedly, and then he holds out my umbrella to a passing woman. "Here you go, Miss."

The woman is tall, with dark hair and a navy blue dress. She's holding her purse above her head in a lame attempt to block the rain. "I couldn't, thank you," she says with a smile, shaking her head. "You two need it as much as I do."

"We'll be fine," says Mr. Flood. "We don't have far to go. Please, take it."

The woman looks at me for approval, but I just shrug. She looks back at Mr. Flood and shakes her head again. "I really couldn't," she says.

But she doesn't walk away.

Mr. Flood steps toward her and presses the umbrella

handle into her grip. "Go ahead," he says. "You're going to need it."

I can tell she feels guilty, but she doesn't try to hand the umbrella back to him. "It's really coming down, isn't it?" she says. "And they weren't even calling for rain tonight."

Mr. Flood nods and backs out from under the umbrella. "They'll really be kicking themselves after tonight," he says.

"Oh, they're always wrong anyway," says the woman. "What's the difference tonight?"

"A couple hundred million gallons," says Mr. Flood, and then he turns and hustles me off across the street.

"An umbrella. What were you thinking?" he says to me angrily. "Get your head in the game, girl. You're supposed to be welcoming the rain, not hiding from it."

I know he's right, but I still pull up the hood of my red raincoat. So I don't like rain, so sue me.

He's lucky I'm out here getting drenched at all, because I *really* don't like rain. In fact, you could say I hate it...which, I know, is totally bizarre given what I'm about to do. Given the power I have.

But hey, you wouldn't like it so much either if your parents died in a flash flood.

As he leads me down Main Street, Mr. Flood taps his twisted cane on the wet sidewalk. It's a special cane that looks like two snakes slithering together, and it has a forked tip at the bottom. Mr. Flood says it's like a divining rod, which he needs to help make the big rains come.

Whenever he walks under a street light, it gets brighter, then goes back to normal when he's past it...though, I don't know, it could be partly because of me. I've got some power, too, even if it's not as much as he has.

Not till later tonight, anyway.

At the end of the block, Mr. Flood drifts over to the corner of City Hall and looks up at a bronze plaque set into the stone wall. The plaque shows the high water mark of the third Johnstown Flood, the one in 1977. It's a couple feet above our heads, and he swings up his cane and taps on it.

High Water

July 20, 1977

8' 6"

"Still my favorite," says Mr. Flood, and then he sighs. "More water in '36, but this one will always be near and dear to my heart." He shakes his head and runs the tip of his cane back and forth over the raised letters on the plaque. "They say it was a once in ten thousand years rainfall. Twelve inches in ten hours.

"Quite an accomplishment," he says, smiling proudly. With his free hand, he plucks the lapel of his powder blue leisure suit with the white piping. As much rain as is dumping down on us both, his polyester jacket and slacks look as dry as if they were still hanging in a closet at home. "Now here I am, wearing the same suit I had on that night back in '77. Getting ready to do it again, and I can hardly wait. How about you?"

"Oh, sure," I say, nodding, though I don't feel anywhere near as pumped as he sounds.

That chicken hawk head of his bobbles a little for no reason, the way it does sometimes these days. "So, how much do you think we'll manage tonight?"

"No idea," I say with a shrug.

"See that plaque up there?" says Mr. Flood, pointing his cane at a plaque mounted much higher than the first.

I nod as I stare up at it.

High Water

March 17, 1936

17'

Grinning, Mr. Flood jabs my shoulder with his bony elbow. "The fourth flood will be higher than that," he says. "See the next plaque up?"

"Yeah," I say, looking at the third and highest plaque, set a few feet higher than the second.

High Water

May 31, 1889

21'

Mr. Flood shakes his soaking wet head. "Higher," he says, his eyes twinkling with amusement.

"Up there," says Mr. Flood, poking his cane at the roof of City Hall. "We'll cover the peaks of the rooftops tonight, and then some. This bowl of a valley down here will fill up like a lake."

I can't take my eyes off the roof. I get a shiver up my spine, and not just because I'm cold and wet. I knew this was going to be the Big Night, but I didn't know just how big it would be.

Mr. Flood chuckles. "Actually," he says, "I guess I should say that the water *would* cover the roof *if* City Hall were still standing after tonight."

"It won't be?" I say.

"Nosiree Dee," says Mr. Flood, and then he swings his cane down and sweeps it in a circle around him. "Matter of fact, not a single thing that you see around you will still be standing in the morning.

"Except that one." With a flourish, he swirls his cane in the air like a sword and points it across Market Street. Right away, I see what he's got in his sights.

When we cross the street to get to it, we're almost run over by two young guys blindly charging full tilt through the rain. One has a newspaper over his head, the other has nothing, and they're both as soaked as if they'd just climbed out of a swimming pool.

Mr. Flood and I stop at the chain link fence around the little grassy square on the corner of Main and Market. The streetlamps brighten when we get close, lighting up a red-painted statue of a big bloodhound inside the fence.

It's Morley's Dog. That's what's going to survive.

A damn statue of a dog.

"I love this dog," says Mr. Flood. "It reminds me why I do this job."

He's lost me with that one. If anything, that dog reminds me of stupidity. People think it's in honor of some hero dog from the 1889 flood, but it's really just a lawn ornament that washed out of some guy's yard.

"This is the true heart of Johnstown," says Mr. Flood, waving his snaky cane at Morley's Dog. "It is battered by the elements again and again, but it survives. It does not surprise or impress, but it endures.

"Just like my perfect little Johnstown," says Mr. Flood. Seemingly as an afterthought, he spits in the grass...and the rain comes down a little harder.

Mr. Flood takes a deep breath like he's drinking in the sweet air of a sunny spring morning, but all I can smell is the rubber-and-soap stink of wet streets.

"God, I love this town," says Mr. Flood. "Always behind the times. Always on a different wavelength than the rest of the world.

"An oasis in an ocean of crap," says Mr. Flood. "And we're the ones who keep it that way." He pats me on the shoulder. "Every forty years or so, we give this town a bath. We wash away its hopes. We wipe the slate clean of so-called progress.

"And Johnstown stays backward and God-fearing, because who knows when the next flood might come around? Johnstown stays small.

"Small as a raindrop." Mr. Flood looks up, straight up, and waves his cane over his head. Just like that, the rain stops falling on us.

I still hear it spattering on the streets and sidewalks, and I still see soaking wet people running past with jackets and newspapers over their heads. I still see it pouring down in sheets through the light of nearby streetlamps...but now, in a circle around us, the rain is frozen in midair. Trails of glistening drops hang suspended between us, shimmering in the glow of street-lamps and headlights.

As much as I hate the rain, this is one of the most beautiful things I have ever seen. I catch my breath, and this time it's not from nervousness.

I never knew. Never knew he could do

This.

One, two, thirty, forty. I can count them. Just hanging there between the sky and the pavement as if someone had paused our disk in the DVD player.

As Mr. Flood reaches out, the droplets part around his arm like a curtain of crystal beads. He slides a pale fingertip under one and holds it there, balanced like a perfect teardrop of blown glass.

"Small as a raindrop," he says. "One raindrop in the midst of a storm."

I reach for my own droplet then, and I catch it on a purple-painted fingernail. I can still hardly believe my eyes, can hardly believe Mr. Flood's frozen the rain. I guess it's not such a stretch, since he and I have some kind of magical rainmaking power.

But still. For some reason, this strikes me as the most incredible thing I have ever seen him do. It amazes me.

It also confuses me. How can he do something amazing like this and then turn around and wipe out a city and its people?

It makes me sad, too, because I can't help thinking about how this man who can do something so beautiful will be dead before this night is over.

MR. FLOOD UNFREEZES THE RAIN AROUND US WITH A snap of his fingers, and the two of us walk down Market Street to Vine Street. By the time we get to the stairway at the end of Vine Street, I have to pee so bad that I'm about ready to wet my pants...but I know better than to ask if I can pee before a flood.

We walk up the concrete steps to an elevated walkway. As we cross over the expressway that loops around the edge of downtown, I'm just glad that the walkway's covered, and I'm out of the rain for a moment.

On the other side of the walkway, we cross a bridge

over the murky, brown Stonycreek River. At the end of the bridge, we enter a little station, and Mr. Flood buys us tickets for the World's Steepest Vehicular Inclined Plane.

"The Incline," as everyone in town calls it, looks like a boxcar that runs up and down the side of a steep hill on railroad tracks. Besides the three floods, the Incline is Johnstown's other claim to fame, though it's not much of one, if you ask me.

"This is some storm we're havin'," says the old man who sells us our tickets. "It's rainin' cats and dogs tonight."

"I heard it'll be raining elephants and dinosaurs before long," says Mr. Flood.

"Might not be a bad idea, headin' for higher ground tonight," says the ticket seller, hiking a thumb toward the top of the hill. "The weatherman on the radio says not to worry, but my rheumatoid knees are tellin' me otherwise."

"I agree with your knees," says Mr. Flood with a wink.

Mr. Flood and I board the Incline passenger car. As the car climbs its track up the hillside, the two of us stand at the window and look out at the rainy city unfolding below us.

Johnstown doesn't look different from most any other night of the year. Rain is one thing that's hardly ever in short supply around here.

Not that it seems to clean the place up very much. I

guess the city was a lot dirtier back in the old days, and it must be cleaner since the steel mills shut down in the '80's...but if you ask me, it still always looks like it has a grimy film over everything. It's like the rain can never wash off this bottom layer of soot that's been stuck to all the buildings and houses and trees and streets since the turn of the century.

Of course, if nothing in town is left standing after tonight (except Morley's Dog), like Mr. Flood says, that grimy soot will finally get scrubbed out the hard way. Unless it all just floats up in the air and comes down and sticks to whatever new buildings are put up after the flood...which, knowing Johnstown, I think is more likely.

When we're midway up the hillside, Mr. Flood elbows me and points to the left and down. I'm not sure what he's pointing at until he tells me.

"The Old Stone Bridge," Mr. Flood says solemnly, wrapping an arm around my shoulders. "Eighty people died in debris that washed up against it in 1889. They burned to death when the debris caught fire. Died by fire because of a flood."

I've heard the story before, but I can't really picture it. All I see is a railroad bridge over the river and expressway on the edge of downtown, an ordinary looking bridge I've been under about a zillion times.

Mr. Flood squeezes my shoulder. "That won't happen tonight," he says. "Drowning only. A merciful death. A peaceful death."

As he says this, I think about my mom and dad, who drowned when a flash flood washed out a bridge under their car. I wish it made me feel better, thinking they might have died peacefully. Unfortunately, I think Mr. Flood is full of crap on this subject.

Sometimes, I can't figure him out. Here's a guy who's about to kill God knows how many people in a so-called natural disaster, and he's patting himself on the back for not burning them to death.

And the messed up part of it is, how much better am I? I can't even stand the thought of my own parents drowning, and here I'm getting ready to help kill hundreds or thousands more in the same exact way.

It's all for a good cause, according to Mr. Flood. Like he said at Morley's Dog, he thinks we're saving Johnstown by wrecking it. He claims that the deaths are the price we pay to protect this place he loves from the craziness in the rest of the world.

It would be nice if I could believe all that like he does. It would be easier if I could convince myself that he's not as crazy as he is powerful, and that I'm not going along with this whole flood thing just because I always do what he tells me. Because I don't want to let him down.

It would be even nicer if I could honestly say that the thought of drowning all those people bothers me more than the thought of one single person dying tonight.

The person who raised me after my parents died. The person who home-schooled me and gave me my powers and taught me to use them. The person whose place I'm supposed to take tonight, just like he took the place of the one before him.

Mr. Flood.

It's funny, because we have kind of a love/hate relationship. He's never let me live my own life. All he's done is push me since Day One to learn the "family business" and take over for him.

But he's never hurt me. I never had to do without. I'm pretty sure he's treated me the same way he'd treat his own kids, if he had any.

There's another reason, too...another reason I don't want to see him die.

When you get right down to it, he's all I've got.

The rain hammers the roof of the boxcar, falling harder than ever. As we climb toward the upper station and the hilltop borough of Westmont, I dread the thought of going out in that downpour.

Mr. Flood swings his cane up and raps the forked tip on the window. As soon as he does it, a lightning flash illuminates the town like an instant of daylight creasing the darkness, blowing back in time from tomorrow morning.

Not that tomorrow morning will be all that bright for Johnstown.

Thunder cracks in the distance, and Mr. Flood chuckles. He raps his cane again, and lightning flares like before.

"Water, water everywhere," he says. "And no one's got an ark."

He yanks back my hood and tousles my hair and brings the lightning and thunder with more raps of his cane, and I wonder.

I wonder if I'll end up crazy like him when I get to be his age.

And I wonder what life will be like without him after tonight.

THE RAIN IS BLASTING DOWN AS MR. FLOOD LEADS ME out of the station at the top of the hill. Pushing through the wind-driven sheets is like being hit in the face with one bucket of water after another.

Walking sideways to cut the resistance, I see the old lady who runs the gift shop lock the shop's door and plunge into the downpour. People stream out of the adjacent restaurant, diners and waiters and waitresses alike rushing out to their cars. The conductor who brought us up the hill dashes past us, soaked to the skin after just a few steps.

Everyone's getting out and hurrying home as the storm gets worse. At this rate, the entire Incline station and restaurant ought to be shut down and empty within minutes. Evacuating the place doesn't make sense, because the high ground up here is one of the safest places to be if a flood hits the valley...but I guess no one really knows for sure what's going to happen next.

Except Mr. Flood and I, of course.

Squinting against the rain, I follow Mr. Flood out onto the cement observation deck that juts out of the hilltop beside the station. I'm all slouched over, but old Mr. Flood just about breaks into a run on his way to the railing at the edge of the deck.

When I come up beside him and look down, I see that the flood is about to begin. The Stonycreek River at the base of the hill is rising fast, filling with rain faster than the current can carry it off.

"We're about to make history," says Mr. Flood, drumming his fingers on the metal rail. "How does it feel to be a part of something that people will still read about and talk about hundreds of years from now?"

I turn to him then, and his eyes are wet with what I think are tears of joy as well as rain, and his pale cheeks are flushed with excitement, and the breath catches in my chest.

"I don't want you to go," I say to him. "Please don't leave me."

Mr. Flood smiles warmly and pats my back. "Thank you," he says. "When my predecessor passed on, I was glad to see her go. It does my heart good knowing that you don't feel that way about me."

As usual, I'm not getting through to him. "Call off the flood," I say. "Let's go home."

"The people of Johnstown are counting on us," says Mr. Flood. "We have to save their way of life."

"Then run for mayor or something!" I tell him.

Mr. Flood tilts his head back and laughs loudly, letting the rain fall into his open mouth. "Hey, I like that!" he says. "A flood elected mayor of Johnstown! That's good!"

"I'm serious," I say, getting more frustrated because I know his mind's made up and it always has been. "Don't do this. Don't go."

"You'll see," says Mr. Flood, brushing my cheek with his fingertips. "When it's your time to pass the torch, you'll understand."

I feel tears in my own eyes, but they aren't tears of joy. I know people would say he's evil and crazy because of what he does--and I guess I couldn't really argue with them--but he's the closest thing I've got to a father. To anyone, actually. I've led a sheltered life, being home-schooled and spending all my time training to flood the city of Johnstown.

"So let's get this show on the road," says Mr. Flood with a giant grin, and then he unzips the fly of his trousers.

Howling like a wolf, he proceeds to pee off the observation deck at the top of the Incline.

As soon as Mr. Flood pees, the rain really cuts loose. It's been raining hard for at least an hour, but that was a trickle compared to the ocean that dumps down now.

When he's done peeing, Mr. Flood tucks himself back in and zips up, then whacks his cane hard against the railing. Immediately, a jagged bolt of lightning lashes down in the heart of the city.

Thunder explodes overhead. As it echoes off the walls of the valley, every electric light in Johnstown except the headlights of the cars on the streets winks out at once.

For a moment, the city is mostly silent and still and dark. Then, through the gushing of the rain, I hear a rising chorus of shouts and car horns. A lone fire siren wails, and then it's joined by another and another. The flashing red and blue lights of fire engines and police cars strobe along the rows of darkened buildings.

This is it, I realize, and my stomach does a somersault.

History in the making.

Mr. Flood whacks his cane on the railing again, and another blast of lightning leaps into the city. As thunder crashes louder than before, he swings the cane up and jabs its two-pronged tip at the sky.

I swear, in the next triple-flash of lightning that sizzles down, the two snakes carved into the cane seem to squirm with a life of their own.

The force of the rain intensifies. The Stonycreek River surges out of its bed, spilling over the sloped, cement flood-control banks that are no better control-ling a flood tonight than they were in '77.

Whooping with joy, Mr. Flood begins to dance.

In the middle of the observation deck, he kicks and gyrates like he's twenty years old instead of ninety. He does the Charleston, the Lindy Hop, the Jitterbug, then shuffles a soft shoe and spins like a whirling dervish. He bobs and stomps like an Indian circling a campfire, shaking his cane like a ceremonial lance.

He twirls the cane like a baton, tosses it in the air and catches it, bouncing the double-pronged tip off the cement. He does a Gene Kelly dance step and slings the cane over his shoulder like an umbrella, singing a song about singing in the rain.

With each move he makes, the rain falls harder.

"Rain, rain, don't go away," shouts Mr. Flood, doing what looks like a cross between the Hustle and a football player's end zone strut. "Give us fifty feet today!"

His magic is strong. I can't believe how fast the flood is growing.

In the valley below us, water rolls from the Stonycreek in wave after wave. Cars slam into each other and strike guardrails and buildings, drivers either blinded by the rain or panicked by the swiftly rising tide.

People and sirens scream like shrieking fireworks. Geysers erupt from the sewers, belching up manhole covers that crash back down onto pavement or parked cars.

And Mr. Flood keeps dancing like a wild man.

Beaming blissfully, he shakes and twirls and jumps

and flaps his arms. The rain comes down harder when he flutters his fingers, and the thunder booms when he stomps his feet.

Looking over the railing, I see that the water is rising steadily down below. Already, the level near the river is higher than car tires, halfway up car doors. Pavement quickly disappears as the streets become canals.

I hear the sound of distant glass shattering. A child screams and dogs yowl like it's the end of the world.

Lights flashing and sirens wailing, emergency vehicles hurtle down the expressway from the townships and boroughs in the surrounding hills.

From somewhere far away, I swear I hear the crack of a gunshot.

I feel a tap on my shoulder then, and I turn to see Mr. Flood bowing deeply, reaching out a hand.

"Will you join me?" he says with a charming smile...too charming for someone about to give up his life.

If I don't help him, I wonder, will anything change? Will he live through the night? Or will he finish the flood without me and die anyway?

It would be easy not to take that hand. It would be easy to refuse to help him kill himself.

It would be easy if I hadn't spent my whole life preparing for this night. If I didn't feel compelled to make him happy.

Especially if whether or not I cooperate doesn't matter, and this is the last night I see him alive.

So I take his hand.

He tosses his cane over the railing and encircles my back with his arm. I follow his lead, looping one arm around him while he raises my other arm high, interlacing his fingers with mine.

Only headlights and the flashing beacons of cop cars and emergency vehicles remain in the valley, but our dance floor on top of the hill is still lit by streetlamps. Windblown curtains of rain pelt down in the lamplight as Mr. Flood leads me in a waltz.

Our feet splash in the water as we glide in a circle, stepping one-two-three, one-two-three, one-two-three. Mr. Flood's sky blue eyes lock with mine, and he laughs out loud and picks up the pace.

Soon, we're moving so fast that the waltz becomes a polka. Mr. Flood steps on my feet once or twice, but he's light as a feather.

I get dizzy from spinning around, and I try to slow down, but he won't let me. I close my eyes for an instant as we keep turning, but it doesn't help. I still feel light-headed.

When I open my eyes, I realize that spinning around isn't the only reason for my light-headedness. As I look down, I see that my feet no longer touch the wet deck.

Mr. Flood and I are dancing on air.

We're floating three feet above the cement. There's nothing under us but air and rain.

I shoot Mr. Flood a look of surprise, and he just winks and keeps hauling me in circles like this is something he does every day. Then, he slows down the polka and tightens his grip on my hand.

"Aphrodite," he says, using my full name and raising his voice over the rushing of the rain. "I give you my power! Use it to continue my sacred work!"

First, I feel a tickle in my fingers, like the start of pins and needles. Then, I feel a mild shock like static electricity buzzing into my palm.

Then comes the real juice. A sudden, searing jolt burns its way up my arm and explodes in my chest like a firework and shoots out into every inch of my body.

I feel like I'm on fire. My entire body quivers and hums like a power line.

And it keeps coming.

It's too much for me. My vision whites out, and my heart jackhammers like I've just downed twenty espressos. Everything seizes up at once, and I can't take a breath.

Then, the current slows, and I start to come out of it. My muscles unclench, and the racing engine in my chest becomes a heart again. I choke down a breath, and my whited-out vision jitters back into color and form and light.

It is only now that I realize we're still waltzing, even

though I've stopped moving my feet. Mr. Flood has been carrying me ever since the first shock of the power transfer crashed through me.

I realize something else, too.

I never knew it before, but until this moment, my senses of sight and hearing and smell and touch and taste have been blocked to the beauty of the rain. Though I've had more sense of rain than other people, and even some influence over it, I've been wrapped in layers of plastic and bound with chains compared to how I am now.

I can see every shimmering pearl of rain as it falls. I can smell the difference between them, tell the exact altitude and part of the country where the source water evaporated to form the cloud that gave birth to each droplet.

I can feel the size and shape of each drop as it hits my skin. I can taste the acid mixed in with the water and pinpoint the air pollutant that produced it.

And I can hear the true song of the rain--not the staccato pattering of showers striking cement and wood and metal, but the vibration of droplets as they stretch and blow and collide, the secret shivering music like millions upon millions of violin strings all playing different notes at once in one heavenly, keening chord.

For the first time in my life, I can see and hear and smell and touch and taste. Everything around me is more amazing than I ever imagined.

And this, I realize, is how Mr. Flood feels every day of his life.

"This is it, Dee," says Mr. Flood, the sound of his voice snapping my focus back to him. He smiles sadly, and I can tell that the rain running down his face is mixed with tears. I know exactly how many raindrops and exactly how many tears. "One big push. The two of us."

This is the moment he's been getting me ready for all my life. The moment when he pours out the last of his power into me, and together we bring down the full force of the flood on Johnstown.

The moment when I lose him.

I know I'm supposed to go along with his plan like I always do. Take all the power and let him drop dead like he did his own predecessor. Watch as our flood drowns the city and feel all proud of myself for making history and saving a way of life.

But what can I say? I guess he didn't do such a good job raising me, because my priorities are all screwed up.

Drowning hundreds of people just doesn't do it for me. My heart just isn't in it.

And as for letting the person I care most about die, well...

Forget it.

Especially now that I'm surging with power and I know how to use it and I finally have a plan of my own.

"Goodbye, Dee," says Mr. Flood, and he pulls my hand in and kisses the knuckles. "Don't let me down."

"I won't," I tell him, though I mean it in a different way than he does. "I promise."

"Then let's show 'em how it's done!" he shouts, thrusting our joined hands high in the air.

Mr. Flood shuts his eyes and knits his brows together in concentration. Electrical arcs spark from his shoulders and arms like tiny bolts of lightning.

Our clasped hands glow blue-white in the rain, then disappear in a flare of light. At the ends of our arms, where our hands should be, all I see is a pulsing ball of energy like a dwarf star dropped down from the heavens.

Once again, I feel the full current of power surging out of him, but this time, it doesn't overwhelm me. My heart races, but I don't convulse, and my vision doesn't white out like before.

This time, I sense the extent of the charge he contains. I know exactly how much he has left and how long it will take to deplete at the rate it's draining into me. In other words, how long until he empties out and dies.

We continue to turn slowly in the air above the deck. At the other end of the crackling circuit we've formed, I feel Mr. Flood reach out with his mind, coaxing me to focus my energies upward.

I do as he wants, extending streams of power like glistening fingers toward the sky. All the while, I divide my attention between the heart of the storm and the level of life-sustaining charge still remaining in Mr. Flood's body.

Together, we massage the clouds like dough, wringing out more water. We reel in fresh clouds from afar and knead them into the thunderheads, heaping up mountains so heavy with rain that they burst at a touch.

The rain blasts down like an emptying ocean. I hear the screams of sirens and people from below, the crash of waves, a distant explosion, but I can't look down. The rain keeps growing stronger, just as Mr. Flood grows weaker and weaker still.

When I feel that his reservoir of power has nearly gone dry, I take control.

His eyes shoot open as he realizes what has happened. Desperately, he reaches through the link and tries to snatch back the reins, but it's too late. I'm too strong for him now.

I take a deep breath.

As I draw the air into my lungs, I pull all the power back inside me. I press it into a ball and hold it there, burning and buzzing and straining against my chest.

I count to three.

Then, I blow out my breath and let loose the power, flinging out a billion sparks in all directions.

Mr. Flood makes a hopeless grab for them with the flicker of strength he has left, but it's not enough. The sparks race everywhere like hypercharged fireflies, leaving glittering trails that hang in the air.

And every single one of those sparks carries a piece of me. I send them whizzing through the rain, chasing off the hillside and out over the valley. They divide again and again as they go, endlessly multiplying, spraying out twinkling constellations under the stormclouds.

Then, when the sky over Johnstown is full of tiny, dancing stars, I pour my power out through them. I do something I saw Mr. Flood do earlier tonight, something amazing.

But I do it on a much bigger scale.

All at once, every falling drop of rain freezes in mid-flight.

The hammering of water on pavement and metal and water suddenly stops. The droplets hang like billions of crystal beads, winking in the strobing red-and-blue light from the cop cars and fire trucks and ambulances. It's just like before, when Mr. Flood froze the rain around us at Morley's Dog...only I've stopped a major storm over an entire city.

And I'm not done yet.

I wait for a handful of heartbeats, touching every single suspended drop with my mind. Turning them.

And then I let them fall again.

Upward. I let them fall upward.

With a roar, every hanging drop of rain pours straight up. Then, every drop that's already hit the ground rushes upward, too.

The flooded streets and parks and rooftops empty

into the sky. Geysers gush up from the windows and doorways of waterlogged buildings. Point Stadium dumps up its watery load like an overturned bowl.

Every drop that has fallen ascends. What came down must go up.

I laugh out loud as it happens. I almost can't believe what I've done. It's like a miracle.

And speaking of miracles, I don't have to pee anymore...even though I never did go to the bathroom.

Here's history in the making. Here's something people will read about and talk about for hundreds of years.

A backward flood. An upside-down flood.

A flood of the sky.

Now *this* is something that will save a way of life. People will want to preserve and study this place, try to figure out what happened without disrupting whatever delicate balance enabled this miracle to occur.

This will save Johnstown. I didn't have to destroy the city and drown hundreds or thousands of people to do it, either.

And I saved someone else, too.

Mr. Flood looks at me, and the tears in his eyes this time are tears of betrayal and confusion and disappointment.

But he'll live. I left him more than enough strength to survive, whether he likes it or not.

He might not be happy now, but sooner or later, he'll

come around to my way of thinking. It only makes sense, right? I mean, why destroy the city every forty years or so when there's a better way?

Here's what I'm thinking:

This might be the first flood of its kind in history.

But it won't be the last.

ABOUT THE AUTHOR

Robert Jeschonek is an envelope-pushing, *USA Today* bestselling author whose fiction, comics, and non-fiction have been published around the world. His stories have appeared in *Clarkesworld, Galaxy's Edge, StarShipSofa, Pulphouse,* and many other publications. He has written official *Star Trek* and *Doctor Who* fiction and has scripted comics for DC, AHOY, and others. His young adult slipstream novel, *My Favorite Band Does Not Exist*, won the Forward National Literature Award and was named one of *Booklist's* Top Ten First Novels for Youth. He also won an International Book Award, a Scribe Award for Best Original Novel, and the grand prize in Pocket Books' Strange New Worlds contest. Visit him online at www.bobscribe.com. You can also find him on Facebook and follow him as @TheFictioneer on Twitter.

WHEELING, WEST VIRGINIA, 2015

Though Cary Beacon knew in his heart that heroic measures would soon be called for, he left behind his super-hero costume. After all, it was only the costume of a make-believe hero from comic books and movies. Cary just wore it to make money by showing up at kids' birthday parties or car dealerships.

It had nothing to do with the fact that he was a real-life super-hero.

He laid the blue tights and red cape on the bed and stared at them for a moment. He would just have to be a hero as he was--bony tall body, red hair streaked blonde, beat-to-hell leather jacket and jeans, red t-shirt with comic book sound effect "POW!" in black block letters in a jagged yellow starburst on the chest. He knew it wouldn't matter what he looked like as long as he managed to save his kids.

Cary stopped staring at the costume and went back to packing. If he wanted to save his kids, he had to hurry.

Well, they weren't really his kids, at least by blood. In fact, the people who had taken them were their actual birth parents, their genuine mommy and daddy.

That didn't mean the kids belonged with them, though.

Cary charged through the trailer, gathering up clothes and odds and ends and pitching them in Wal-Mart shopping bags. His ex-girlfriend, Crystal Shade, had taken the suitcases at the same time she'd taken the kids.

Cary shouldered the screen door open, raced down the battered wooden steps, and chucked his loaded shopping bags into the back seat of his taxi. Without closing the car's door, he bolted back inside the trailer to grab a few last things.

He bagged what little food was left in the place, which amounted to a jar of peanut butter, half a loaf of bread, two apples, and three cans of SpaghettiOs. He yanked the sheets, blankets, and pillow from the bed and threw them in the cab, too. Beyond that, Crystal had pretty much cleaned the place out. While Cary had been hard at work driving fares around town, she'd been stealing the kids he loved and everything he owned.

Almost everything.

Kneeling in the rear corner of the bedroom, Cary peeled up the stubbly gray carpet. Jamming the blade of his pocket knife into a crack in the floor, he pried up a square of plywood.

Sweat ran down his back and sides as he reached into the hole and drew out a manila envelope. He undid the clasp and folded back the flap, then pushed his hand inside.

He pulled out a rubber-banded wad of money and dropped it on the carpet, then reached back in to fish out what he really wanted.

As his fingers closed around the familiar shape, he felt a surge of relief. Crystal hadn't taken everything, hadn't even found this hiding place.

Super-heroes need good hiding places because they've got so much to hide.

Crystal didn't even know the Starbeam Ring existed. Cary had lived with her for over a year, and he'd never shown it to her or even mentioned it.

Thank God thank God thank God.

Holding up the ring, he watched the light gleam on its faceted surface. To the uninitiated, it might look like a hunk-a-junk kids' toy from a gumball machine, molded from see-through blue plastic.

Only Cary and the rest of his super-hero teammates, the Nuclear Family, would know better. They would know at a glance that this was a Starbeam Ring, said to bestow super powers on its wearer.

Not that any of them would believe that the ring really did bestow powers...except Cary, that is.

The rest of the Nuclear Family--Cary's brother and two sisters--all had rings of their own. They all agreed that their father, who had given them the rings in the first place, had made up the story of the Starbeam Rings just to stoke their imaginations when they were kids.

"When you need your powers most, they will come to you," their father had told them solemnly, back before the oldest of them had turned ten. "Always remember that when the chips are down, your secret powers will save the day."

The others had stopped believing, but not Cary. He still thought that when he truly needed his powers the most, the ring would activate them. Even though they had let him down before, again and again, he still believed.

Even though, years ago, when he'd never needed them more, they'd failed him...and someone he'd loved had paid the price.

This time won't be like before. Nobody dies this time.

He slid the ring onto the only finger small enough to fit through it--his left pinky. He stuffed the wad of bills, his secret savings, back into the manila envelope, and got to his feet.

Just then, his cell phone rang.

Pulling it from the pocket of his bluejeans, Cary stared at the glowing blue caller I.D. screen embedded in the shell. Instantly, he recognized the number displayed there.

It was the number of the cell phone he'd given little Glo for her birthday a month ago, in case of emergency. The phone he'd made her promise to keep secret from her mother, who'd been starting to make him suspicious.

He snapped his phone open and pressed it to his ear. "Hello?" He kept his voice low so the caller would be the only one to hear it.

"Help." The voice on the line was midway between a whisper and a squeak. "Please help us."

Cary had a thousand questions, but he knew the little girl wouldn't be able to talk for long. "Where are you, Glo?"

"Bathroom." Glo sounded like she was on the verge of breaking into sobs. "At the airport."

Rage swirled deep in Cary's heart. Crystal had planned her escape well. "Which airport?"

"Arizona somewhere." Glo paused, and Cary heard a woman's voice in the background. "Gotta go!" she said. "Mommy's calling."

"Is Late okay?" said Cary.

"Yeah," said Glo. "Bye!"

"Call next time you have a chance," Cary said quickly. "Don't let them find your phone."

He wasn't sure if Glo had heard him, because the call was dead by then.

As he closed the phone and slid it back into his pocket, he wished that Glo had given him more details about her location. At least he knew that she and her brother, Late, were okay.

For the moment, anyway. The key now was to catch up before the monster could hurt them...the monster otherwise known as Crystal's new boyfriend, Drill. He was also her boyfriend from years ago, long before Cary came along.

And he was Glo and Late's father...but no less a monster for having brought such great kids into the world.

Just thinking about Drill and what he might do to Glo and Late was enough to throw Cary into high gear. He didn't even take the time for a last look around the trailer on his way out.

He switched off the lights and darted outside, letting the screen door bang shut behind him. He didn't bother locking the door, because nothing of value was left inside.

Nothing mattered anymore except the kids, and saving them from the bad guys.

As much of a rush as he was in, Cary hesitated once he got behind the wheel of his cab. For a moment, as he thought about the job ahead of him, he felt overwhelmed.

Crystal and Drill had a huge head start. Cary didn't

even know exactly where they were. Drill, especially, was tough enough that he'd probably kick Cary's ass if he *did* catch up to them.

Looks like a job for the Nuclear Family.

Unfortunately, as much as Cary would've loved having some Nuclear Family backup, he knew it wasn't coming. His brothers and sisters had abandoned the super-hero life long ago. Cary had held out hope for a reunion longer than any of them, but even he had finally given up on the team.

His brothers and sisters just didn't care about being super-heroes anymore. The fate of Glo and Late was up to him and him alone.

Cary took a deep breath and gripped the steering wheel.

Only The Hurry can come to the rescue this time! Don't miss this pulse-pounding solo adventure of the Nuclear Family's own human sonic boom!

With a steely gaze and a grim expression, he threw the cab into gear and stomped on the accelerator. Gravel spun out from under the tires as the car leaped away from the trailer and hurtled off down the road at more than twice the legal speed limit.

LILLY, PENNSYLVANIA: SATURDAY, APRIL 5, 1924, 7:30 PM

One hour before the power was cut and all the lights went out in the town of Lilly, Olenka Pankowski shivered as she watched the white-robed men pile out of the train. One after another, they poured from the five coaches and onto the platform, melting together into a shifting sea of white.

Except for the stomping and scraping of their feet on the coach steps and platform, the robed men were silent. Every one of them wore a conical hood with a flap drawn up in front, leaving only the eyes visible through a rectangular slit.

And they just kept coming.

"How many *are* there?" whispered Olenka's friend, Renata Petrilli. Like Olenka, Renata was seventeen, and her father and brothers worked in the coal mines.

"Dozens." Olenka pushed a lock of jet black hair behind her ear. "Dozens and dozens."

Renata's pudgy fingers tightened on Olenka's arm. "People were saying they'd come, but no one said there'd be so many."

Olenka watched with wide, dark eyes as more of the robed men stepped off the train and into the swarm of white. "Maybe more of them than there are of us."

"But why so many?" said Renata.

Dominick Campitelli, who stood just in front of them

in the crowd of townspeople, spoke over his shoulder. He was just a year older than the two of them and was already at work in the mines.

"Because they're afraid of us," he said, pitching his voice well above a whisper...loud enough for the robed men to hear it. "Because every time they send some guys to burn a cross here, we send 'em runnin' back with their tails between their skirts."

"But what about this time?" said Renata. "There's so many of them."

Dominick snorted. "This time, too. Wait and see."

Olenka wasn't so sure he knew what he was talking about. As she watched, the robed men continued to stream from the train. She'd lost count of how many had debarked already, but she thought there must be at least a hundred of them.

A fear that she hadn't felt for years began to build in her chest. A storm was coming, the kind of storm she remembered too well from her early childhood in Poland.

She recognized the signs. Something terrible was about to happen.

"This is bad," Mrs. Froelich said behind her. "Why won't the union just take back their men? The Klan's only here because the mineworkers threw out the Klansmen."

Mrs. Lorenzo, who was standing on the other side of Renata, turned around. "That's not the only reason they're here, and you know it."

"You don't know what you're talking about," said Mrs. Froelich.

Father Stanislavski looked back at Olenka and nodded. "They're here because they hate us," he said

matter-of-factly. "The Wops and the Polacks and the Hunkies take their jobs."

"Bah," said Mrs. Froelich. "You got a prosecution complex."

Olenka watched the robed men as they lined up on the platform. She thought Father Stanislavski was more right than Mrs. Froelich gave him credit for.

Directed by two men with more decorations on their robes than the others, the Klansmen arranged themselves into four columns stretching the length of the platform. They looked like an army, ready to march, their ranks continually swelled by the white-clad comrades who kept flowing from the train.

Not for the first time, Olenka thought about hurrying home before whatever was going to happen got started. She knew she wasn't safe there. If a storm started--*when* the storm started--the robed men would surely be at the heart of it.

Then again, she had a feeling that nowhere in her tiny town would be safe that night. She didn't really think it would make much difference whether she was out in the open or locked away in her family's rooms two blocks away.

On the platform, the two leaders walked between the

columns, talking to the lined-up men. As the leaders passed, the men undid the ties that held their masks in place and lowered the flaps, exposing their faces.

Most of the men looked straight ahead, like soldiers in formation, but some of them glanced at the townspeople. Olenka couldn't see all of them, and she didn't recognize the ones she could see. They might as well have left their masks in place, as far as she was concerned; to her, the cold, stern expressions of the strangers looked as unreadable and inhuman as the masks.

She had seen those expressions before, on other men who came in the night. She had seen them in the village her family had abandoned over a decade ago, back in Poland.

When the leaders had finished walking the length of the lineup, they returned to the front of the group. Standing a little apart from the others, the two men talked in low voices and looked at their wristwatches. The train conductor stepped down from the locomotive to join them.

"What's happening?" said Renata. "What are they talking about?"

Olenka shrugged. The conductor pulled a pocket watch on a chain out of his vest pocket. He flipped open the cover and looked at the face of the watch, then said something to the two robed leaders.

The three of them walked down the stairs from the platform and crossed the track of the siding on which the train sat. For an instant, Olenka thought the men were heading for the crowd...but they rounded the locomotive instead and stood along the main track, gazing in the direction from which the train had come a half hour before.

As the leaders and conductor stared along the track and checked their watches and talked some more, Olenka looked back at the men on the platform. Draped in white, they stood at attention, maintaining their rigid columns like statues.

Waiting.

In front of Olenka, Dominick Campitelli and Nicolo Genovese talked in hushed voices, but not so hushed that she couldn't hear what they were saying.

"They can hide a lot under those damn robes," said Dominick. "I bet they've got plenty of guns."

"Pistols," said Nicolo. "Knives, I bet."

"They must think we're pretty dumb," said Dominick, "if they think we don't have 'em, too."

Olenka's mouth was dry. The palms of her hands were damp with sweat.

She could feel it. The storm was closing in.

Turning, she scanned the crowd for her father, Josef, but didn't see him. She wondered where he was; though she had come straight from Renata's home to the station and had not seen her father since the train's arrival, she had no doubt that he knew what was happening. Lilly was too small a town for word not to have reached him.

And Josef was too much a man of action not to be doing something about this.

All the more reason for her to worry when he was nowhere in sight at such a dangerous moment.

"What are they waiting for?" said Renata.

"Maybe they're havin' second thoughts," Dominick said loudly. "Maybe they're gonna hitch up their skirts and go home."

Some of the people in the crowd laughed, but not Olenka. Not Father Stanislavski, either. He looked back at her and shook his head slowly.

"Not yet," he said, as if his words were meant for her alone. "They won't leave until they're done with us."

Olenka shivered.

"The big bad KKK," said Dominick. "Looks like a bunch of sissies to me."

"Hey, you!" a young man from the back of the crowd hollered up at the men on the platform. "Yeah, you! With the white hat on! I think you need a little more starch in them bedsheets next time!"

Most of the crowd laughed. The blanket of anxiety that had lain over them since the train's arrival seemed finally to have lifted.

"Don't'cha know you're not supposed to wear white before Memorial Day?" shouted another young man.

"No, no," said someone else. "Those are wedding gowns! They're gettin' married!"

"If those are the *brides*," yelled a woman, "I'd sure

hate to see the *grooms*!"

Just about everyone laughed at that one.

And then, they all stopped.

The whole crowd turned as one to stare out along the track in the direction that the conductor and Klan leaders were looking. Everyone had heard the same thing at the same moment.

A distant, high-pitched toot. And there it was again.

"Oh my God," said Renata.

The second one had been closer than the first.

The third was closer yet.

Father Stanislavski turned and nodded knowingly at Olenka. "This is what they were waiting for."

Like everyone else, Olenka knew what it was. She had heard it thousands of times before, by day and by night...but never with such a feeling of dread.

It was the whistle of an approaching train.

Fifteen minutes later, the train pulled onto the siding behind the first train and unloaded another hundred white-robed men.

Fifteen minutes after that, every electric light in the town of Lilly went out at once.

What happens next? Find out in The Masked Family, now available for your favorite e-reading app or device!